KEY
HUNTERS

THE
HAUNTED HOWL

KEY HUNTERS

*Getting lost in a good book
has never been this dangerous!*

THE MYSTERIOUS MOONSTONE

THE SPY'S SECRET

THE HAUNTED HOWL

KEY HUNTERS

THE HAUNTED HOWL

by Eric Luper

Illustrated by Lisa K. Weber

SCHOLASTIC INC.

> For my critique partners: Loree, Liza, and Kate.
> It's been fifteen years and still no fluff.

Text copyright © 2016 by Eric Luper.
Illustrations by Lisa K. Weber, copyright © 2016 by Scholastic Inc.

All rights reserved. Published by Scholastic Inc., *Publishers since 1920*. SCHOLASTIC and associated logos are trademarks and/or registered trademarks of Scholastic Inc.

Library of Congress Cataloging-in-Publication Data

Names: Luper, Eric, author. | Weber, Lisa K., illustrator.
Title: The haunted howl / by Eric Luper ; illustrated by Lisa K. Weber.
Description: New York : Scholastic Inc., 2016. | Series: Key hunters ; 3 |Summary: In their third trip through the enchanted library, Cleo and Evan land in "The Werewolf's Curse" where Evan is promptly bitten by a werewolf, and the two need to find the cure—and the next key—before the full moon rises and Evan becomes stuck in this horror story forever.
Identifiers: LCCN 2016013773 (print) | LCCN 2016015218 (ebook) | ISBN 9780545822114 (pbk.)
Subjects: LCSH: Books and reading—Juvenile fiction. | Libraries—Juvenile fiction. | Librarians—Juvenile fiction. | Magic—Juvenile fiction. | Werewolves—Juvenile fiction. | Locks and keys—Juvenile fiction. | Adventure stories. | CYAC: Books and reading—Fiction. | Libraries—Fiction. | Librarians—Fiction. | Magic—Fiction. | Werewolves—Fiction. | Locks and keys—Fiction. | Adventure and adventurers—Fiction. | GSAFD: Adventure fiction.
Classification: LCC PZ7.L979135 Hau 2016 (print) | LCC PZ7.L979135 (ebook) | DDC 813.6 [Fic]—dc23
LC record available at https://lccn.loc.gov/2016013773

10 9 8 7 6 5 4 3 2   16 17 18 19 20

Printed in the U.S.A.   40
First printing 2016

Book design by Mary Claire Cruz

CHAPTER 1

"Have you seen Ms. Crowley today?" Evan asked Cleo across the library table.

"No," Cleo said. "It's weird because she's usually hanging around with her clicky high heels and her screechy voice."

They were already halfway through recess, and Evan and Cleo had a job to do. They needed to get another step closer to finding their former librarian, Ms. Hilliard, who had mysteriously disappeared into one of the magical books in the secret library beneath their school.

"What are you working on?" Cleo asked.

Evan pushed away his book. "A gross report."

"What's gross about it?"

"It's about bats," Evan said. "Few things scare me more than bats."

"Have you ever seen a live bat up close?"

"I don't need to see one up close to know they're gross."

Cleo looked at the book. "They're kind of cute, like dwarf hamsters. I'd call this one Moe and that one Sprinkles."

"I'd call *you* crazy."

"I'd call me bored," Cleo said. "Let's go."

Evan and Cleo found their way to the farthest shelf in the darkest corner of the library—to the shelf that hid the secret door that led to the magical library. Cleo laced her fingers and boosted up Evan until he was eye level with a huge, dusty, boring-looking book titled *Literature: Elements and Genre from Antiquity to Modern-Day.*

Before Evan could pull out the book, Cleo groaned and lowered him back to the floor.

"What's the matter?" Evan asked.

"My shoulders are sore from Ansley Teal's birthday party last night."

"Your shoulders are sore from a birthday party?" Evan asked.

"The party was at Adventure Time Rock Gym. Rock climbing is really hard. We learned all about rappelling and harnesses and carabiners."

Evan pretended to know what she was talking about. He rolled a stool over, climbed up, and pulled on the book. It tipped forward and the secret bookcase swung open. The stairway that led to the hidden room under their school library was darker than usual.

"Don't you think it's weird that Ms. Crowley isn't around?" Evan asked as they went down.

"Maybe she's on break or something," Cleo said.

The magical library was darker than Evan remembered. Shelves, sliding ladders, and spiral staircases stretched into the darkness above them. Catwalks and balconies reached around corners and across gaps to let readers explore every nook. At the back of the library, over a stone fireplace, hung a tapestry that showed an open book with people swirling into it among a sea of colorful letters. The fireplace was already lit, but dimmer than usual.

"Does the library look creepy today?" Evan asked.

Cleo shrugged. "It always looks creepy to me."

They snuck along the library wall. Evan pulled out the key they had gotten on their last adventure. It was the key to a fancy sports car given to them by the head of a secret spy organization.

"Which book do you think it unlocks?" Evan asked.

"I don't know. Why don't we ask the woman in that painting?"

They looked at the painting that hung just above them. Evan didn't remember ever seeing it hanging there before. It showed a woman wearing a yellow dress and a crown. Her eyes seemed to follow them wherever they moved.

Suddenly, the canvas of the painting began to stretch toward them. The woman's hands reached out from the painting and swiped at them.

Cleo let loose a scream. Then she and Evan ran.

They climbed a ladder and darted across a catwalk. But when they hurried around a corner, they bumped straight into their current librarian, Ms. Crowley.

"I've been waiting to grab that key from you!" she said. She reached for Cleo, but Cleo ducked.

The kids slid down a brass pole, and that's when they spotted it. A locked book lay on the table in the center of the room. The cover was made of cracked leather and covered in cobwebs. The title read *The Werewolf's Curse.*

"Give me the key," Cleo said.

"I am *not* going into a werewolf story," Evan said.

"You want to rescue Ms. Hilliard, right?"

Ms. Crowley was already sliding down the pole, her sharp heels scraping against the metal. "Come here!" she screeched. "I need that key!"

Evan shifted from one foot to the other.

He had told Cleo that few things scared him more than bats. Werewolves were one of those things.

But then he thought about Ms. Hilliard. She needed their help.

Evan handed Cleo the key.

"Don't go without me!" Ms. Crowley cried.

Cleo jammed the key into the lock and turned it. The lock popped open. Letters burst from the pages of the book like a thousand crazy spiders. They tumbled in the air around them and began to spell words. The words turned into sentences, the sentences paragraphs. Before long, they could barely see through the letter confetti.

Then everything went black.

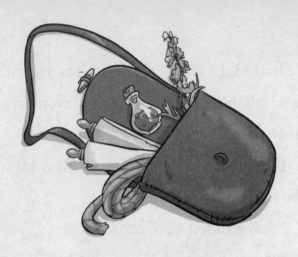

CHAPTER 2

Pain burned deep in Evan's arm. Sweat trickled down his forehead. He opened his eyes. He was lying on a bed in a dim shack. Cleo and a boy Evan didn't recognize stood over him. Cleo's hair was pulled back. She was wearing a plain gray dress with a white apron. The boy's skin was pale and looked paper-thin.

"Who . . . are you?" Evan asked.

"The fever has clouded his mind," the boy said. "We must act quickly."

Cleo touched Evan's cheek. "What fever?"

"He has been bitten."

"Bitten?" Evan said. "Like by a mosquito?"

The boy looked stern. "Evan, you've been bitten by a werewolf."

"How do you know my name?" Evan asked.

The boy looked worried. "It's me, Francis, son of the village doctor. You're Evan, the baker's son, and this is Cleo, the blacksmith's daughter. We've been friends since we were tots."

Evan thought the word "tot" sounded funny. He chuckled and began to sit up, but dizziness overcame him and he lay back down.

"If I hadn't pulled you into my family's home, the mob would have gotten you," Francis said.

"What mob?"

"The *angry* mob, of course," Francis said. "Tonight is the full moon. At midnight, you'll undergo your first transformation. It won't be easy."

Evan shook his head. "I really don't think—"

Francis grabbed Evan's arm and rolled up the sleeve. A burning line of red dots circled his forearm near his elbow.

"You were bitten," Francis said. "Some say getting *eaten* by a werewolf is better than being *bitten* by one."

Cleo peeked out the curtains. "It's already getting dark," she said. "Should we tie Evan to the bed and stay with him until morning?"

"I'm afraid that won't work," Francis said. "When he transforms, the bed will break into splinters and the rope torn to bits . . . along with us."

"Seriously, guys," Evan said, sitting up. "I'm feeling better . . ."

Evan stopped. He sniffed at the air. He could smell the oil from the dim lamp, the earthy wool of the blanket, the stale hay inside the mattress, all in more detail than he could ever remember noticing.

"Weird," Evan whispered.

Evan sniffed again. The hairs on his neck stood up. He smelled swampy mud and nervous sweat. He heard shallow breathing. There was someone behind the door.

Evan sprang from the bed. He surprised himself by how far he was able to leap. He landed softly, took two steps, and flung open the door. A hunched figure disappeared around the corner of the building.

"We can't stay here," Francis said. He loaded an empty jar, some papers, a coil of rope, and a few other supplies into a leather bag and slung it over his shoulder.

"What do we do?" Evan asked.

"There is a way to get rid of the werewolf inside you," Francis said.

"Call animal control?" Cleo asked.

"No. A cure," Francis said. "We need to find leaves of wolfsbane, sprinkle it into water collected from a flowing stream, and stir it

14

with the silver Lycan Spoon under the light of a full moon."

"I'm turning into a werewolf in a few hours and you want to throw a tea party?" Evan said.

"It's more like a potion."

"How do you know all this stuff?" Cleo asked.

"My father studied it for years. Everyone said he was crazy—that it was too dangerous—but he wanted to end this curse once and for all."

"Where's your father now?" Evan asked.

A tear rolled down Francis's cheek. "You already know this," Francis said. "My father disappeared several months ago. He left the village to confront the werewolves with his cure. He hasn't been back since."

"I'm guessing there aren't any wolfsbane shops in this village," Cleo said.

Francis reached past her and flung open the curtains.

"We'll find it there," he said, pointing into the darkness.

A flash of lightning lit the night. An old mansion sat atop a rocky mountain. A single, jagged path led up to it through a dark forest.

"We must gather the wolfsbane in the haunted cemetery," Francis said. "Then, we climb the path. It is said there is a waterfall nearby where we can collect our water. Finally, we'll find the spoon inside the mansion's crumbling walls."

"Why can't we use any old spoon?" Evan asked. "That house looks creepy."

"The Lycan Spoon has special powers. It was crafted from the leg bone of the first werewolf."

"Uh . . . gross," Cleo said.

"It's the only thing that will save Evan," Francis said. "The road to the old mansion is dangerous. But the mansion itself contains horrors that would make the bravest man weep."

"So why are you helping us?" Evan asked.

"I need to finish my father's work," Francis said. "It's the only way to save the village. Plus, we've been friends since we were tots."

"You're going to have to stop saying 'tots,'" Evan said.

Something howled in the distance. The

sound echoed around them, then disappeared in the night. Another howl rang out, this one closer.

"Come," Francis said. "We must be quick."

CHAPTER 3

The moon peeked from behind the clouds, lighting the streets of the village. Francis led Evan and Cleo along a narrow alleyway until they came to a stack of firewood. They crouched down behind it.

"That mansion is an evil place!" a man called out. He had a round belly, and spit flew out of his mouth with each word. He stood on a platform facing a group of townspeople who held torches and pitchforks. "Now Evan, the baker's son, has been bitten. He can't be allowed to remain. It isn't safe for anyone. We need to end this once and for all!"

The crowd roared angrily.

"It's Old Man Jameson," Francis whispered. "He thinks he runs this village. Even though we're close to a cure, he thinks killing the werewolves is the only solution."

"Sounds like he's a few sandwiches short of a picnic," Cleo said.

Evan sniffed the air. Old Man Jameson stank like rotten eggs and feet. "He's also short a few bars of soap."

"What's a picnic or soap got to do with any of this?" Francis said.

A low growl came from the back of Evan's throat.

"What was that?" Cleo asked.

"The transformation is beginning," Francis explained. "We must hurry."

As they turned to go, Cleo bumped the firewood. A single log tumbled down. Then another. Suddenly, the whole pile collapsed.

Everyone in the town square turned to look.

"Run," Francis said.

"The baker's son!" Old Man Jameson screamed. "GET THEM!"

The kids bolted. They ran down a side street, then made a few quick turns as Francis led them along a twisted alley. He pointed at a large crate and put his finger over his mouth to quiet them. They ducked behind it just in time.

Seconds later, the mob thundered past as the townsfolk searched for Evan. Angry voices echoed through the night. Evan shrank deeper into the shadows until the glow of their torches faded.

"You can't hide from us forever!" Old Man Jameson called from a distance. "We need to end this curse once and for all!"

"We *will* end it," Francis muttered, "but not with pitchforks and torches."

"Actually, pitchforks and torches sound better than brewing tea," Evan said.

"Never underestimate the power of a good cup of tea. Now, follow me. I know a secret way out of the village."

Francis led them down another alley. They climbed a wall and squeezed between the posts of an old fence. Finally, they came to a bridge that crossed a deep gully. On the far side, the branches of the forest were so low

and thick they blocked the path. The night was silent, as though every cricket was holding its breath.

"Once we begin, there will be no turning back," Francis said.

"What choice do we have?" Cleo asked.

"We could wait until midnight and let me snack on those villagers back there," Evan offered. "They seem kind of mean."

"They're frightened and upset," Francis said. "Most of them have lost friends or family to the jaws of a werewolf."

Cleo's eyes narrowed. "Then our mission is clear."

As they approached the path, the thick branches parted like giant, bony hands. And just as soon as they crossed into the forest, the branches fell back into place, sealing them inside.

"I guess you were right," Evan said to Francis.

"About what?"

Evan tried to see the bridge or the lights from the village behind them. There was only darkness. "There really is no turning back."

CHAPTER 4

The path twisted up the moonlit mountain. It seemed like it was never going to end. Finally, they came upon an iron gate. Beyond, Evan could see headstones jutting from the ground at every angle.

"This looks scary," Evan said.

Cleo glanced around. "Everything in this whole weird book is scary."

"We have no time for books," said Francis.

"The wolfsbane grows in this cemetery. My father wrote about it in his papers."

Cleo grabbed the bars of the gate and tugged. It creaked open.

"I guess we go in," Evan said.

They made their way through the cemetery, weaving around crooked statues and low stone buildings. An owl hooted and fluttered from a gnarled tree.

"Maybe we should split up," Francis offered. "We can search for the plant more quickly that way."

"Are you nuts?" Evan said. "Whenever people split up in a horror movie—"

Cleo stepped on Evan's foot. "He just means there is safety in numbers."

"Perhaps you're right," Francis said.

They walked along a gravel trail until Cleo suddenly stopped. "Did you ever get the feeling you were being watched?"

"All the time," Evan said. "How else would my mom know when I don't wash my face in the morning?"

"Because you *never* wash your face in the morning," Cleo said.

"Ha!" Francis said. "And you don't have enough sandwiches for a picnic!"

Cleo rolled her eyes. "That's not how that saying goes," she said. "Now, be quiet. I think someone is watching us."

Evan sniffed at the air. The hair on the back of his neck stood up. He peered into the darkness. On the top of a grassy hill, in a cluster of trees, something glowed.

"There," he whispered.

Francis stepped forward. "Show yourself," he called out.

The glow disappeared.

"We're not afraid!" Francis said.

"Speak for yourself," Cleo muttered.

Leaves rustled. Branches scraped together. Soon the glow reappeared behind a knot of bushes. And it was not alone.

Three more glowing figures floated behind a headstone to their left.

"I tell you, we're not afraid!" Francis yelled.

A breathy whisper sounded right behind them. *"You will be . . ."*

They spun around.

Nothing.

"Let's just find the wolfsbane and get out of here," Cleo said.

But when they turned to go, something stopped them dead in their tracks.

Standing—no, floating—in front of them was a woman in a flowing dress. She glowed an eerie white. Evan could see right through her. And something about her seemed familiar. Several other glowing figures floated up behind her.

"Every soul ever taken by a werewolf haunts these woods," the ghost said.

"Haunts . . . these . . . woods . . ." the other figures echoed.

"Every month during the full moon, the werewolves raid the village," the ghost said. "Every month, they add to our numbers."

"Add to our numbers . . ." a few others whispered.

More ghostly figures drifted down from

the trees and began swirling around them. Evan felt like he was in a spooky blender.

"There is no escape," the first ghost wailed.

"No . . . escape . . ." the others repeated.

"Can't you make one exception?" Evan asked.

"No exceptions," the ghost said.

"Then, we have no choice . . ." Francis said. "Run!"

Evan, Cleo, and Francis ran up the trail as fast as they could. The ghosts laughed as they swooped around them. Each time one would come close, the hair on Evan's arms bristled.

The trail led them across a rickety bridge into a dark meadow.

"Look," Cleo said. "The trail continues on the other side!"

They started across the field. The ghosts swirled around them, coming closer all the time. The kids were getting really scared, and soon found themselves back-to-back, surrounded by the frightening spirits.

"What are you going to do to us?" Evan asked.

"Look at the trees . . ." one of the ghosts hissed.

Evan squinted into the darkness. Dozens of skeletons hung from the branches.

"You may not pass," a ghost wailed. "If a single living soul makes it out of the cemetery, we will be trapped in these woods forever."

"Aren't you already trapped in these woods forever?" Francis asked.

"If the head werewolf of the pack is destroyed, our souls will be released."

"That's what we plan to do," Evan said. "We're going to rid this land of the werewolves."

Suddenly, the mass of spirits parted and a single ghost floated forward. It was the woman they had seen earlier. Her long hair was twisted into a bundle on the top of her head. Now that Evan got a closer look, she looked a lot like Cleo.

"I was hoping you'd stay away," she whispered. She reached out her hand and tried to brush Cleo's cheek, but her fingers passed through Cleo's face. Cleo shuddered and the figure began to weep.

Francis stood. "Who are you?"

"I'm Miriam, Cleo's mother," the ghost said. "A werewolf took me many years ago, not long after Cleo was born."

"She's not *really* my mother," Cleo whispered. "My mom would never wear her hair like that. This must be a book thing."

"Then, I guess we have to play along," Evan said.

Cleo stood. "Mother," she said. "Evan, Francis, and I are going to the mansion to defeat the werewolves."

"It cannot be done," Miriam said. The ghosts crowded closer around Francis, Evan, and Cleo.

"We can do it," Cleo said. "Francis knows the cure and . . . well . . . if we don't, Evan will become a werewolf by midnight. We have no choice. We just need some wolfsbane."

Miriam thought about it for a moment, and then floated into the air. She turned to face the other ghosts. "Let them pass," she said.

"But if they fail—" one of the ghosts hissed.

"If they fail, we are doomed to these woods forever," she cut in, "but if we never let anyone pass, we doom ourselves."

The ghosts dimmed.

"There is the wolfsbane you seek." Cleo's mom pointed to a cluster of low purple flowers on the hillside. "Take what you need and continue on your journey."

Evan tried to pull some of the wolfsbane, but as soon as he touched the plant, a fiery pain shot up his arm. He fell to his knees.

"You can't touch it," Francis said as he cut a bunch and stuffed it into his bag. "If it's not prepared properly, wolfsbane is deadly to anyone afflicted with the werewolf's curse."

Evan rubbed his hand. "You could have

told me that sooner," he said. "I guess I'll just hold the bag for you."

As Evan and Francis gathered the wolfsbane, Cleo walked through the dark meadow, her ghostly mother at her side.

"You've grown so much," Miriam said to Cleo. "It's been years, but I'd recognize you anywhere."

Cleo wasn't sure what to say to a mother she'd never met before, so she made some things up. "It's been tough, but Dad and I are getting along fine. He's been doing . . . blacksmith things . . . I've been going to school."

"You seem keen on this Evan," Miriam said. "Are you interested in him?"

"Eww, gross, Mom," Cleo said.

"There's nothing gross about it. I was your age when I met your father. Plus, Evan's family owns the bakery. Their family can offer you—"

"Mom, Evan and I are just friends."

Miriam floated a little higher. "I believe that's what I said when my mother had this same talk with me."

"Seriously, can we talk about something else? Like maybe how you and your ghost friends can help us?"

Miriam glowed a little more dimly. "I'm afraid I've done all I can by letting you pass through the cursed forest."

"I understand," said Cleo. She wanted to reach out to her book mother, but she knew it was no use. You can't hug a ghost.

"I really hope you don't join me here," Miriam said. "If you fail, we'll be trapped forever."

"Forever is a long time," Cleo said.

Miriam closed her ghostly eyes. "A very long time," she said.

A wolf's howl pierced the night.

"We'd better go," Cleo said.

CHAPTER 5

The trail led out of the cemetery and along the walls of a rocky gorge. The kids made their way along narrow ledges and across moss-covered bridges that zigzagged over a stream far below.

"Running water," Cleo said. "We need some to make the cure."

Evan peered down. He hated heights, and

the sight of all those boulders looking so tiny made him dizzy.

"It's too far," Francis said. "We'll find a closer spot."

They hiked farther up the mountain. Soon they came to a lookout point that jutted out into the gorge. A stone railing lined the edge. Evan was glad the railing was there. Without it, it'd be easy to fall off the cliff.

Cleo leaned over and spotted a waterfall cascading down the cliffside into a dark pool below them.

"This is as close as we're going to get," she said.

"We're still too high up," Francis said.

"I can get down there," Cleo said. "Gimme the coil of rope you packed."

Francis pulled it out of his bag and handed it over. Cleo wrapped it around her waist, looped it under her thighs, and tied a complicated knot. She took the jar from Francis's bag and stuffed it into the folds of her dress. "Lower me down. As soon as I get the water, pull me back up. Simple."

"Nothing in these books is ever simple," Evan said.

"Just lower me down there."

Evan doubted he could hold Cleo by himself, but Francis was bigger than he was. The two of them together would be able to do it.

As they lowered her, Cleo tapped her feet against the cliff walls. Cleo knew from the Adventure Time Rock Gym that it was a lot easier to be lowered than to climb up. With Evan and Francis on the other end of the rope, all she had to do was lean back and walk down the walls.

When she was near the bottom, Cleo called to the boys. "Hold on!"

She pulled out the jar and scooped up some water. Ripples spread around her. She flipped the lid closed and snapped the metal clamp.

She was about to call to them to pull her up when she saw something beneath the surface. It was a face—a young boy's face. He couldn't have been more than four or five.

His dark eyes looked sad and his voice sounded like gentle violins. "Help me . . ."

Cleo stared back. "Who are you?"

"Please help me."

Cleo knew it wasn't a good idea, but some-thing about the small boy's voice drew her in—and he needed her help. This boy was in trouble. She leaned down.

"Closer," the boy beckoned. "Loosen your rope."

Cleo's hands went to her waist.

"What's taking so long?" Evan called from above, but Cleo barely heard him. It was as though he and the rest of the world were far away.

Cleo knew the water would be cold, but something about the boy made it seem warm and inviting. She reached her hand toward the surface of the water, toward the boy.

The boy lifted his hand. "Just a little closer. Help me."

When their hands were almost palm-to-palm at the surface of the pool, Evan tugged impatiently on the rope. Cleo bounced. She shook her head and blinked. The boy was enchanting her! Cleo began to slip out of the rope she had loosened.

Suddenly, the boy's eyes glowed green, and he hissed. His pale face turned the color of seaweed and he bared a mouthful of needle-sharp fangs. A slimy claw burst from the water and grabbed Cleo's wrist.

The rope yanked forward. Evan's feet slid on the mossy stone. Francis's hands scraped against stone, and he let go. He fell to the ground, hitting his head on the railing and collapsing in a heap. Without Francis's help, the rope began to slide through Evan's fingers. Something was pulling on it—hard.

A scream rose from the pool. Evan knew Cleo was tough. She must be really scared of something. And now he was scared, too, because she'd gone totally silent.

Evan slid forward and rammed into the railing. He looked down. A glistening green sea creature had its tentacles wrapped around Cleo. It thrashed underneath the surface of the water.

"What is that thing?" Evan screamed above the roar of the waterfall.

Cleo's head came up. "Does it matter? Pull me up!"

The rope slid farther through Evan's fingers. He strained to hold on, but his palms burned and his shoulders felt like they were going to give out. He squeezed the rope tighter and pulled with all his might. His arms bulged. His back muscles rippled, stretching his shirt tight. Claws sprouted from his fingertips. Evan let out a beastly howl and heaved on the rope.

The sea creature sputtered as Cleo slipped from its slimy grasp. "Come with me to the depths and eternal sleep!" it hissed.

"I'm not much of a napper," Cleo said, kicking at the creature.

Hand over hand, Evan pulled Cleo up. She spun her body around and worked her feet against the rock wall. The sea creature began to climb after her.

"You *will* join me!" it spat.

Suddenly, they heard a cackle. Evan and Cleo looked up and saw a figure at the top of the gorge. Her body was misshapen. One leg dragged behind her. She leaned her hunched shoulder against a large rock and pushed. Stones began to tumble down toward them.

"You'll never reach the mansion alive!" the woman screeched.

Evan recognized the voice. It was Ms. Crowley!

One stone, then another, fell past Evan. Cleo saw them coming. Like a kung fu master, she ran sideways across the cliff face, using her rope as a swing. The rocks plummeted past her and struck the hideous sea creature. But the creature kept climbing.

"I'll get you!" it hissed.

With a wink, Ms. Crowley launched another stone at them, this one much larger than the first ones. Cleo twisted out of the way, and the boulder only grazed her shoulder. Was Ms. Crowley trying to kill her or save her?

The sea creature wasn't as fast as Cleo. It let out a terrible shriek as the boulder knocked it off the cliffside and into the pool below. It thrashed around, but soon disappeared into the water.

Evan pulled on the rope in one big heave. Lifting Cleo was easier than he remembered. Cleo grabbed the railing and swung her legs over it. She looked up just in time to see Ms. Crowley disappearing in the distance.

Cleo shook her head. "That was close," she said.

"Too close," Evan said.

Francis slowly opened his eyes. "What happened?" he asked as he dusted himself off. "Actually, we don't have time. Midnight will soon be upon us and . . ." His words trailed off as he looked at Evan.

"What?" Evan asked. He looked down. His arms were covered in thick fur. Inch-long black claws stuck out of his fingertips.

"I guess I need a manicure," he said.

"And maybe some laser spa treatments," Cleo added.

"We need to get to the mansion," Francis said. "We must find the silver Lycan Spoon before it's too late."

"Uh, guys," Cleo said. "That might be harder than we thought."

They looked where Cleo was pointing. The bridge to the other side of the gorge was out.

CHAPTER 6

"The falling rocks must have destroyed the bridge," Francis said. "It's more than twenty feet to the other side."

Evan remembered how he had been able to spring out of bed earlier. He was full of energy and felt stronger than he ever had before. Maybe he could make the jump. Somehow, it didn't seem so far.

"Give me the rope," he said.

"You can't do it," Cleo said. "It's too dangerous."

"It's only dangerous if I fall . . . and I won't."

Evan grabbed the end of the rope and clenched it between his teeth. "Tie the other end to that tree," he told Cleo. "Pull it tight."

She scrambled up a few boulders to a small cluster of skinny trees and tied the rope around the thickest one. "What now?"

Evan growled his answer. He took a running start and leaped into open air. Even with his newfound werewolf powers, it was a long stretch. The far side of the gorge came at him quickly, but not quickly enough. Evan wasn't going to make it. He stretched as far as he could, but his fingertips barely reached the ledge. His claws dug into the stone, leaving deep scratch marks. His left hand started to slip, but Evan held on. He dangled over the deep gorge.

"Pull yourself up!" Francis yelled.

"Duh," Evan tried to say, but his voice was muffled by the rope. He climbed onto the ledge and tied the rope around a large stone. The rope slanted up across the gorge to where his friends were standing.

"It's like a zip line," he said.

"I didn't do the zip line at the rock gym," Cleo said. "The wait was too long."

"Well, now's your chance."

Cleo grinned. She grabbed Francis's bag and looped the strap over the rope. Without another thought, she pushed off. She slid across with amazing speed and landed on the ledge next to Evan.

"I like this Evan better than the normal one," she said.

"What's the difference?"

"This one's brave and confident."

"I'm always brave and confident," Evan said.

"Um . . . I can think of a few things that I bet still spook you."

"What do I do?" Francis called from the other side of the gorge.

"Take off your sash," Evan said. "Loop the sleeve over the rope."

Francis did as Evan suggested. Then he shut his eyes and shoved off. The tree behind him groaned and bent forward. Wood snapped and the tree gave way. The rope dipped. Francis grabbed it as he fell.

Evan and Cleo heard him slam against the cliff below them. They scrambled to the edge. Francis was barely hanging on, but his sash was a lost cause. It landed in the stream below and rushed away.

"I'll pull you up!" Evan called down.

"I'm too heavy!" Francis said.

"You're too heavy for the old Evan. This is new and improved werewolf Evan!" He tugged on the rope.

"You're doing it," Cleo said. "Get him a little higher and I'll grab his shirt."

They worked in silence until Francis was safely by their side.

Suddenly, a distant screeching filled the air. Then came the roar of ten thousand beating wings. The screeching got louder. The moonlight dimmed as a black patch filled the sky.

"That's a weird-looking cloud," Cleo said.

Evan squinted at it. The cloud was moving as though it had a life of its own. It jerked left, then right. His hands began to tremble. "I . . . don't think . . . that's a cloud," he said.

The dark thing soared overhead and then dipped into the gorge. Within seconds, thousands of bats swarmed around them. The screeches were deafening. Furry, fanged creatures slapped into them.

Evan's hands flew up to guard his face. His screams were almost as loud as the bats themselves. He swatted at the air as the bats flapped and clawed their way past the kids.

By the time the screeches faded into the distance, Evan was crouched against the rock wall, his hands over his head.

"Brave and confident, huh?" Cleo said.

"Those bats were way creepier than Moe and Sprinkles!" Evan said.

"A cowardly werewolf. That's funny," Francis said. "Now, let's hurry. There isn't much time left."

The moon lit their way. They climbed out of the gorge and followed the path to the top of the mountain. Dead trees rose from the rocky, barren ground. Ahead of them, the mansion loomed. It was dark except for a single lit window on the top floor.

"Interesting," Evan said.

"What?" Cleo asked.

"I would've thought it would be raining right now."

"Why?" Cleo asked.

"It always rains when people come across a creepy mansion."

Lightning flashed. Droplets began to fall. The night turned cold and stormy. Francis, Evan, and Cleo ran toward the mansion. The entrance gaped open—the heavy door had been splintered and busted off its hinges.

"The werewolf pack did this," Francis said. "They must be inside."

"How many are there?" Evan asked.

"No one knows for sure," Francis said.

"So, even if we defeat the head werewolf and cure Evan, we will still have to face more of them?" Cleo asked.

"I hadn't thought about that," Francis said.

Evan sniffed around the door. He could smell the scent of dozens of wolflike creatures, each one a clear fingerprint in his mind. He could also smell Ms. Crowley's perfume. His senses were getting sharper.

"We may have more trouble," Cleo said. She pointed down the mountain.

Through the storm, they could see a mob of people charging up a trail. Their torches were tiny fireflies in the distance.

"The villagers think they can take on the werewolves," Francis said. "If we don't end this by midnight, they're all doomed."

Cleo shrugged. "Old Man Jameson isn't the nicest guy in the world."

Francis glared at her. "Those people are

our neighbors," he said. "They're worried someone they care about will be next."

Evan stood tall. "Then this ends tonight."

He walked through the gaping doorway into the darkness.

That's when something pounced on him.

CHAPTER 7

It was Ms. Crowley—sort of. Even at full height, she was shorter than Evan. Her right shoulder was hunched and her face was puffy and twisted. Her bad leg could barely hold her up. But it was definitely Ms. Crowley.

"Why do you get all the good roles in these books?" she asked.

"I think you're cute," Cleo said. "I want a stuffed animal of you!"

Ms. Crowley scowled. "I'm the assistant to the mad scientist who lives in this mansion. He studies werewolves, and his recent experiments have transformed him into one. His name is Dr. Thorne."

"Father," Francis said. "I knew it."

"Your father is the head werewolf?" Evan asked.

"You can't find a cure unless you come dangerously close to the disease," Francis said.

"There's no time to lose," Ms. Crowley said. "If you want to find the Lycan Spoon, follow me."

"Why should we trust you?" Evan said. "You dropped a bunch of boulders on us!"

"I hit that sea creature. If it weren't for me, Cleo would be gone forever."

"She's on *our* side?" Francis said.

Ms. Crowley's mouth opened, then closed again.

"I used to give her stale bread from my father's bakery in the village," Evan explained.

"Uh, yeah," Ms. Crowley said. "I owe my life to Evan and his bread-baking family."

Evan wasn't sure Francis was convinced, but they didn't have a moment to spare. Midnight was approaching.

Francis, Evan, and Cleo followed Ms. Crowley up a wide staircase. Old oil paintings covered the walls. Cobwebs hung like thick curtains. Evan was sure a woman in one of the paintings was staring at him. Her eyes followed him as he took each step.

A deep, muffled laugh came from behind the wall.

Evan thought about the painting in the magic library. "We should hurry."

"We need to cross the ballroom, cut through the library, and climb to the tower."

"That doesn't seem too tough," Cleo said.

Ms. Crowley peered at Cleo. "Just you wait," she said mysteriously.

At the top of the stairs, they started down a long hall. Francis rushed ahead and flung open the two wide doors to the ballroom. The moon peeked through a high window, giving everything an eerie, blue glow. Large tapestries covered the walls, and dark suits of armor lined each side.

Francis started into the room. But as soon as he stepped near the first suit of armor—*SQUEAK!*—it leaped forward, swinging a spiked club wildly. Francis ducked just in time.

"Ahhh!" Evan cried. "Crazy alive armor!"

"I thought you were supposed to be brave and confident!" Cleo ran into the ballroom and barreled straight into the armor. It busted into pieces and scattered across the floor. The club slid into the corner.

"Oh, that looks easy," Francis said. He rushed forward and slammed into another suit of armor. This one flew apart, too.

Four more suits of armor marched from their places to block them.

"No one passes," one of the suits of armor declared. It held a huge sword.

Ms. Crowley snuck around behind the armor and crouched down. When Cleo

slammed her shoulder into the armor, it fell back, toppling over Ms. Crowley. It smashed to the floor and broke into pieces.

The three remaining suits of armor began to advance. Six more fell in behind them.

"They're easy to beat, but there are too many of them!" Cleo said.

Evan's eyes darted from one suit of armor to the next. Each held a weapon, and they were all coming at him and his friends. He took a deep breath. His heart was racing. Suddenly, he bolted forward. He snarled and leaped. The next seconds were a blur of claws and teeth. Before long, he was sitting on a pile of torn metal and broken weapons.

"Whoa," Cleo said.

"What did I do?" Evan asked.

"You turned feral," Francis said. "You're becoming more and more like a wild wolf."

"Watch out!" Ms. Crowley screamed.

A suit of armor with no legs had crawled up behind Evan. It had pushed itself up and lifted a battle-ax. Evan shrank back. It was hard to be brave on purpose.

But Cleo had his back. She ran forward and kicked the helmet across the ballroom. Then the rest of the armor and the battle-ax collapsed into a pile.

"That was some kick," Francis said.

"I guess five years of soccer and seven years of karate is good for something," Cleo said.

"Remind me to thank your parents for

doubling up on your after-school activities," Evan said.

A mix between a scream and a howl echoed through the room.

"Hurry!" Francis insisted. "The transformations have begun!"

CHAPTER 8

Ms. Crowley led them into a huge chamber with more cobwebs than before. When Evan's eyes adjusted to the darkness, he could make out rows of dusty shelves. Catwalks and balconies lined the walls above them. They stepped over a broken sliding ladder and walked past an unlit fireplace. Above it hung a familiar-looking tapestry. Evan couldn't believe what he was seeing.

"You didn't think the only magic library in the world was underneath your elementary school, did you?" Ms. Crowley said.

"Who would want to come visit this terrible place?" Evan asked.

"All places deserve to be studied," Ms. Crowley said. "Truly talented librarians can travel at will between magic libraries to different places and times."

"I'll bet that's what Ms. Hilliard did," Evan said. "If there ever was a talented librarian, it was her."

Ms. Crowley tensed. "I'm afraid that's not what happened," she said.

"Then what *did* happen?" Cleo asked.

"Let's just say she broke a librarian's most important rule: Keep track of where things go, including yourself. Now, stay sharp."

A figure shifted in the shadows.

"Have you come . . . in search . . . of a book?" a withered voice said.

An ancient-looking woman hobbled over to them. She wore a hooded robe and held herself up with a walking stick.

"So much to read, so much to learn," the librarian muttered. "Let me help you find what you need."

"We'd love to spend time in your library," Evan said, "but—"

"But what?" the woman barked. "You must read. How else will you learn all you wish to know?"

"Ask someone?" Cleo said.

The woman glared. Her eyes were red pinpricks that glowed in their sockets. She stepped closer. "We've not had a visitor in years," she said. "So much to read, so much to learn."

"We're in a rush," Francis said. "We're in search of the Lycan Spoon."

"The Lycan Spoon," the woman said. Her eyes shifted toward the shelves above them. "Never heard of it."

"Well, if you can't help us, I'm afraid we've got to be moving along," said Cleo.

The old woman hooted. "Nonsense. You will stay. There is so very much you need to learn."

The woman lifted her arms. Her robe blew back and a nest of white hair tumbled around her shoulders. Books began flying from the shelves.

"Run!" Ms. Crowley said. "I'll stop her!"

"NO TALKING IN THE LIBRARY!" the woman cackled. She rose into the air and the books began swirling around her. She lifted an arm toward Ms. Crowley, and the books shot at her like arrows.

Ms. Crowley ducked under a table and rolled to the other side. The avalanche of books missed her by inches, pelting the table-top with heavy thumps.

Evan, Cleo, and Francis bolted toward the door.

"Hold on a second," Evan said. "That crazy librarian looked up when we mentioned the Lycan Spoon. Maybe it really *is* here."

"Why would a spoon be in a library?" Cleo asked. "If there's no talking in the library, I'm sure there's no *eating* here, either!"

More books flew from the shelves and began swirling around the librarian.

"Libraries sometimes collect things other than books," Evan said. "They collect music or scrolls. There's a library in Canada that collects puppets."

"Puppets are creepy," Cleo said.

"Not as creepy as that librarian!" Evan said. "Follow me." He ran to a ladder and began to climb. Cleo climbed after him.

"That is the Restricted Area!" the librarian screeched. She waved her arm, and the ladder slid Cleo and Evan along the rails, slamming them into a wall. "Those shelves are off-limits!"

Francis climbed onto a table and leaped to one of the catwalks. "Where was she looking?" he called down.

"Over there!" Evan pointed to a platform suspended from the ceiling by thick chains.

Francis ran along the catwalk. But with a wave of the librarian's arm, the path began to shift away from the platform. Francis ran faster, but by the time he got to the end, he was too far away to jump.

Evan looked above the platform. The chains ran through four pulleys. They stretched across the high ceiling and into the wall. Far below, at floor level, he saw a lever.

Evan bounded across the library and sprang into the air.

"Don't touch that!" the librarian yelled. "It's a Restricted Lever!"

But it was too late. Evan grabbed the lever and yanked. *Clank! Clank! Clank!* The platform shifted and began to lower.

"Do not meddle with my collection!" the librarian said. She turned to Evan and pointed her walking stick. The books swirling in the air around her dove right for him.

Evan braced himself, but knew that if the heavy books hit him, it wouldn't end well.

Suddenly, someone screamed a battle cry.

It was Ms. Crowley. She was pushing a hefty wooden book cart across the library, right at the creepy, old librarian. Ms. Crowley smashed into her with a loud thud. All at once, the books dropped lifelessly to the ground.

Ms. Crowley stood over the librarian and crossed her arms. "As soon as you stop giving a book your attention, it loses its power," she said.

"How . . . How did you know that?" the librarian said.

"Because I'm Barbara Crowley, librarian."

The platform came to rest on the library floor. In the center stood a pedestal that held a gleaming silver spoon with a bone handle.

A tear ran down the old librarian's cheek. "It's been so long . . ." she said. "My name is Mary Cutler Fairchild. I'm a librarian, too. I traveled here nearly a century ago. And I've been here ever since."

"Why did you attack us?" asked Evan.

"This mansion is a dangerous place. A mad doctor came here many moons ago. He raids my library and takes what he needs for his nasty experiments."

Francis looked pale as he climbed down from the catwalk. "How do you keep the werewolves away?" he asked.

The woman waved her hand. The books that had been scattered across the floor rose into the air and returned to their places on the shelves. "They only come once a month," she said. "I do pretty well defending myself."

"We saw," Cleo said.

"Why do you need the Lycan Spoon?" Mrs. Fairchild asked.

"The spoon has the power to mix a potent cure," said Francis. "We are going to end the werewolf's curse once and for all."

"I've heard the legends," Mrs. Fairchild said.

Francis opened his bag and pulled out a fistful of leaves. "The legends are true," he said.

Mrs. Fairchild grinned. "Let's get started."

CHAPTER 9

Francis and Mrs. Fairchild set to work on the potion. Francis used his father's notes, which he had tucked away in his bag. Any time they needed further information, Mrs. Fairchild waved her hand and a book flew to them from the shelves.

"Three sprigs of wolfsbane, not four," Mrs. Fairchild said.

"Sixteen stirs with the spoon," Francis said.

As the moon rose higher in the night sky, they heard a howling from above.

"That sounds close," Cleo said.

"Midnight is upon us," Mrs. Fairchild said over her shoulder.

Suddenly, pain shot through Evan's spine. He fell to the floor and began writhing around.

He looked to Cleo. "Help me!" he whispered. His arms began to lengthen and a tail sprouted from his backside. His face stretched into a snout, and the shiny brown fur that had dotted his arms grew thick and spread all over him.

"The potion will soon be finished!" Francis called out.

But soon wasn't soon enough. Evan let out a bloodcurdling howl and sprang up. He bounded across the library and crashed through the door. The ground was light under his feet, and he could sense dozens of creatures on the roof above him. He ran up the stairs and leaped outside.

A man wearing a stained lab coat and glasses paced in front of a pack of half-wolf, half-human creatures. Evan knew it was Dr. Thorne. "Tonight is the night," the man said. "We will destroy the village! Our pack will grow in number and strength. Tonight, we claim this land for the werewolf!"

"Father, this is madness!" Francis shouted as he and Cleo ran out onto the roof. He held a jar filled with purple liquid. "I have found the cure. We can all go home."

"Why would I want a cure?" Dr. Thorne

growled. "Men are weak. Wolves are strong!" The werewolf pack began to circle them.

Lightning crashed. Rain pelted down around them. Two torches lobbed up from below and landed on the roof. Soon flames began to rise all around them.

"The villagers are setting fire to the mansion!" Cleo said.

"It makes no difference," Dr. Thorne said. "In moments we will destroy them and take our place at the top of the food chain!"

"Actually, it's a food web," Cleo said. "We learned about it in science."

She took a quick count. "Let's see," Cleo said. "Twenty werewolves and a mad scientist against a bunch of kids and an angry mob. You'd better get some more werewolves."

Dr. Thorne chuckled. "I think you've miscounted, little girl." He turned toward the moon. His eyes glowed yellow. His limbs stretched, a gray tail sprouted from his backside, and his nose lengthened into a snout. "Twenty-one werewolves!" he growled. "And I'm the strongest of them all!"

Evan couldn't control himself. He bounded forward and pounced on Dr. Thorne. They wrestled to the ground, snarling and barking at each other like vicious dogs. They twisted, thrashed, and clawed. Dr. Thorne was much larger, but Evan was quicker. Both were out for blood.

The other werewolves began circling Cleo and Francis.

"Fresh meat," said one of the werewolves.

"Children are so sweet and tender," another growled.

"Where's your hunchback friend now?" Francis said to Cleo. "I told you she couldn't be trusted."

The werewolves began closing in.

Just then, something pelted the werewolves from above. It was a flying book! One after another they rained down upon the pack.

"Time to check out!" Mrs. Fairchild cackled from the doorway.

The werewolves yelped and shrank back. It was just the break Francis and Cleo needed. They ran to Dr. Thorne and Evan, their feet slipping on the slick roof.

"Father!" Francis called over the pelting rain. "I have the cure right here!"

But Dr. Thorne and Evan were wrapped around each other, a furry whirlwind of snarls and gnashes and claw swipes.

Francis stepped closer.

Evan and Dr. Thorne whipped around and crashed into him. The potion flew from Francis's hand over the edge of the roof.

Cleo darted forward and leaped into the rainy night. As she sailed over the edge of the roof, she grabbed Francis's sleeve. She reached out her other hand and snatched the jar just before she fell and slammed against the side of the mansion.

Cleo dangled by one arm. She glanced down. It was a long fall to the ground. The villagers waved their pitchforks as the fire spread. Flames licked at her feet. Francis's sleeve began to tear as he tried to get a hold of her.

"You're . . . too heavy for me," Francis said.

"Maybe I can help." It was Ms. Crowley. "I may be small, but I'm freakishly strong."

She reached past Francis, grabbed Cleo's wrist, and pulled her onto the roof.

"Thanks," Cleo said. She swirled the potion in the jar. "Now, how are we going to get Dr. Thorne to drink the potion when he doesn't want to?"

"I have an idea." Francis tore off the rest of his sleeve.

CHAPTER 10

Evan wasn't sure how long he would last against Dr. Thorne. He could dodge most of the blows, but it was only a matter of time before the evil werewolf got lucky. He needed to try something new.

He slipped away and bounded to the other side of the roof. He scaled a chimney and leaped to another ledge. He could hear the shouts of the villagers below.

"You don't have to fight me," Dr. Thorne growled. "Feel how powerful you've become. Join us!"

Evan felt the pull of the mad doctor's words. He'd never felt strong or fast or unique in any way. The thought of leaving this world and going back to being plain old ordinary Evan started to seem unappealing. He lowered his arms.

But it was a trick. Evan was helpless . . . and Dr. Thorne pounced, pinning Evan's arms.

"Every pack has a few weak links," he snarled. "It's my job to break them."

He tilted his head back and howled at the moon.

That's when Cleo jumped up and stuffed Francis's balled-up sleeve into Dr. Thorne's mouth. It was soaked in purple liquid, which dripped down the werewolf's snout.

Dr. Thorne screamed. He dropped to his knees as his body began to change. His arms and legs shortened. His furry tail shrank away. His eyes turned from yellow back to brown. After a long moment, he turned to the kids with a serious look on his face.

"Thank you," he said. "The madness that comes with becoming a werewolf clouded my mind. You saved me." He sat up. "Now that I've been cured . . . the other werewolves have no leader. Watch out!"

Cleo, Francis, and Ms. Crowley turned around. The pack advanced, their teeth bared.

Evan leaped between them and snarled.

"I'm not sure I can hold them off for long," he said.

"I'm not sure you can hold them off at all," Cleo said.

Suddenly, a distant moan filled the air. Hundreds of glowing lights swirled up the mountainside. They swept through the gorge, past the angry villagers, and up the sides of the mansion, snuffing out the fire. The ghosts from the cemetery! They circled the rooftop, then each in turn passed through the potion in Francis's hand. The ghosts were now filled with the cure. Their white glow melted into a light purple, and they dove at the werewolves, flying straight through each one's chest. The werewolves fell to the ground and transformed back into humans.

Miriam glided forward. "You have freed us," she said. "The power the werewolves took from us has been returned, and we can move on."

"Where will you go?" Cleo asked.

"There are worlds beyond this one. We will each find our own path." Cleo's mother turned and floated over to Evan, who was crouched on the edge of the roof. "It is because of your bravery that we have been freed," she said. "You have a choice to make: Keep your werewolf powers or become an ordinary boy again."

Evan thought about it. It was tempting to keep his powers—to stay strong and quick and ferocious—but he didn't like losing control. "I think I'll turn back to how I used to be."

Miriam smiled. "Wise decision."

She placed her hand on Evan's chest. His heart raced and his body twisted. Then, he dropped to the ground. When he opened his eyes, he was back to his regular self.

Miriam turned to Cleo. "Farewell," she said. "You are an amazing young woman."

Cleo knew Miriam wasn't really her mother, but her eyes welled with tears anyway.

Then, all at once, the glowing ghosts flew up into the night sky and disappeared. The rain stopped, the clouds parted, and the moon cast pale-blue light over everything.

Dr. Thorne rested against a chimney. "I'm so sorry for all of this," he said. "Having all that power . . . I couldn't control myself."

Francis knelt beside him. "It's okay, Father."

"It's not okay. I've brought terrible evil upon the village. But I will make things right. Here . . ." He fished into his pocket and pulled out a brass key. "This opens a secret door in my lab. You can escape unseen. I'll talk to Old Man Jameson."

He tossed the key into the air. No one grabbed it, and the key fell to the roof.

Evan looked to Cleo and Ms. Crowley. He knew grabbing the key would send them home, but still he hesitated. "We need to wait for Mrs. Fairchild," he said.

"After what she did to help us, we can't leave her here," Cleo said.

Ms. Crowley nodded.

Mrs. Fairchild hobbled out onto the roof and poked at the key with her walking stick. "I've lived here more than a hundred years," she said. "This is more my home than any-place I've ever lived. Go on ahead. Now that the werewolves are no more, I'll be all right." She knelt beside Dr. Thorne. "Anyhow, I know someone who's going to need me," she said. "You can't rebuild a village without a proper library."

"Okay," Francis said. "Let's grab that key and get out of here."

"Wait," Mrs. Fairchild called out. "Another came through here not long ago. She left a message."

The hair on Evan's neck bristled. "Why didn't you tell us earlier?"

"Because you had not come to the end of this adventure yet," Mrs. Fairchild said. "When you are traveling through a book, there is no room for distraction. The woman's name was Ms. Hilliard. She asked that you not try to find her. She said that the next book, the book this key will lead you to, is the most dangerous you've faced. She said awesome and terrible creatures await you there."

"Thank you," Evan said. "We'll keep that in mind."

Cleo patted Evan on the back. "Sometimes friendship is worth facing a little danger for," she said.

Mrs. Fairchild smiled. "Then, I wish you well, young travelers."

Evan, Cleo, and Ms. Crowley reached out and grabbed the brass key together.

Letters burst from the key like a thousand crazy spiders. The letters tumbled in the air around them and began to spell words. The words became sentences, the sentences paragraphs. Before long, they could barely see through the letter confetti, and then everything went black.

CHAPTER 11

"It's nice to have my old spine back," Ms. Crowley said, standing at her full height. She stretched in front of the fireplace.

Evan looked around. He and Cleo sat at one of the tables in the magic library under their school. Evan looked at his hands. They seemed normal: no claws, no fur. In fact, being a werewolf felt like a dream.

A thick book lay open in front of Cleo. She looked down at it.

"Whoa," Cleo said, scanning the page. "Mary Cutler Fairchild. She was a real librarian. She worked with Melvil Dewey, the guy who invented the Dewey decimal system. She's in the Library Hall of Fame."

"There's a Library Hall of Fame?" Evan asked.

"It's important to honor those who have come before us," Ms. Crowley said.

"Ms. Hilliard knows we're trying to find her," Cleo said. "That's really cool."

"But she warned that awesome and terrible creatures await us," Evan said.

"Awesome is good," Cleo said. "Maybe it's a family of rainbow unicorns that grant wishes and have a gumdrop palace in the clouds."

"I think she meant awesome in the bad way," Evan said. "Like inspiring fear and dread."

"Oh," Cleo said. "That's *not* good."

"It's time we talked," Ms. Crowley said. She walked around the table and sat across from them.

Evan clutched the key tightly. It pulsed in his hands. "You're not taking this from us."

"I know that," she said. "But we will be going into the next book together. Sleep well tonight, because high adventure awaits when we enter our next story."

Evan's arms ached. His back was sore. The thought of entering another adventure so soon made his head spin.

"Why do you want to travel with us so badly?" Cleo asked. "All along you've been mean to us."

"Because you make good companions. You work well under pressure and you're both quick-witted and brave. I know it's no excuse, but I've been nasty because I'm under a great deal of stress."

"What sort of stress?" Evan asked.

Ms. Crowley wrung her hands together and puffed out a breath. "The truth is that I need to find Ms. Hilliard more than you do. She's my sister."

The Lost Library is full of exciting—and dangerous—books! And Evan and Cleo have a magical key to open one of them. Where will they end up next? Read on for a sneak peek of *The Wizard's War*!

Evan and Cleo found themselves in the grand hall of a run-down castle. Light streamed through tall windows. Torn tapestries hung from the walls. Chairs and tables lay broken in pieces. Ms. Crowley was nowhere to be seen. As they looked around, a serious voice broke the silence.

"My name is Vixa," a girl said.

Evan and Cleo spun to face her. She wore a red cloak over a suit of armor. A sword hung from her belt and a silver headband with a glowing red gem circled her head. "I am aide to Tannis, adviser to King Ledipus, ruler of the Kingdom of Bissel. We need your help. Follow me."

"I'm already confused," Cleo said. She wore a leather vest with metal studs and soft boots. Her ears were pointy at the tops.

"You're an elf!" Evan said.

Cleo felt her ears. "I'm a confused elf," she said. "King who? Aide to what?"

"Fantasy books can be confusing," Evan whispered. He wore blue robes decorated with gold stars and moons, and a pointed hat that flopped over. A leather pouch hung from his belt. "Sometimes the strange names are enough to make me want to stop reading. Just stick with it."

"It's not like we have a choice," Cleo said. "Hey, where's Ms. Crowley?"

"She must be somewhere else in the book."

Evan dug through his pouch. Small vials lined the bag. Several scrolls were stuffed alongside them. He figured he must be a wizard.

"Wizard. Rogue," Vixa said, already half-way down the hall. "Follow me. Time is short."

"I'm a rogue?" Cleo asked.

"Of course you're a rogue," Evan said. "Look at your outfit."

"Sweet," Cleo said. "What's a rogue?"

"It's like a thief and an acrobat mixed together."

"Double sweet!"

They followed Vixa to a dark chamber. A withered man wearing a crown slumped on a throne. A hooded man crouched at his side. Vixa looked at the king with concern.

"Good, you've come," the hooded man said. "The king has an important matter to discuss with you." He whispered in the king's ear. The king's mouth quivered. A tiny moan rattled out.

"His majesty has fallen ill," the man said. "I am Tannis, the king's trusted adviser. I will help him tell you what we need."

"What's the trouble?" Cleo said.

"You rogues are all alike," Tannis said. "Always getting right to business."

"Well, most of these books have a problem that needs to be solved," Cleo said.

"Most of these whats?" Tannis asked.

"She means the *world* has many problems that need solving," Evan said.

"Very true." Tannis circled to the other side of the throne and put his ear to the king's mouth. "The king would like you to make peace with the wood elves. Vixa will be your guide."

"What's the trouble with the wood elves?" Evan asked.

"They have waged war against us."

Vixa placed her hand on her sword. "The elves feel we have taken their land. They attack our traders as punishment."

"Well, did you?" Evan asked.

"Did we what?" Tannis said.

"Did you take their land?"

"We cut down a few trees," Tannis said. "The wood elves think all forests belong to them. And their allies, the dwarves, try to claim our underground mines as their own. That's why we've had to bring in the trolls to oversee their work. The Kingdom of Bissel needs resources to prosper. We cannot be distracted by jealous creatures."

"I'm more confused than ever," Cleo whispered.

Evan hushed her.

"This war needs to end," Vixa said, "especially with rumor of the Golden Dragon awakening."

"The Golden Dragon?" Evan asked.

"Have you never heard of the Golden Dragon?" Vixa looked shocked. "She's the most fearsome beast the land has ever seen. Larger than a mountain. Fiery breath that can melt solid stone."

"Standing together, there is a chance we may defeat the dragon," Tannis said. "If we remain divided, we are all doomed."

"Doomed is bad," Cleo said.

"We must travel across the plains, through a mountain pass, and into the dark forest," Vixa said.

Cleo brightened. "That seems okay."

"The journey will be filled with foul beasts," Tannis added.

"Ew," Evan said.

"This should be a simple matter for a clever rogue and a powerful wizard," Vixa said. The glowing gem on her headband dimmed for a moment and she blinked her eyes.

Tannis waved his hand and the gem glowed brightly again.

"You must meet with the queen of the wood elves," Tannis said. "Offer her peace if she will join us. It is the only way we'll defeat the Golden Dragon and save both our kingdoms."

The king moaned and Tannis murmured in his ear. "Now, go," Tannis said. "There's no time to lose."

Evan wanted to help. Clearly, this kingdom *needed* help. But something didn't feel right.

"What's in it for us?" Cleo asked.

"What are you doing?" Evan whispered.

"If I'm a rogue, I should act like one."

"Spoken like a true scoundrel," Tannis said. He held out a silver goblet. It was filled with gemstones of all colors. "Make peace with the elves and you can have as much treasure as you can carry."

Cleo sunk her hand into the fancy cup. As the gems trickled through her fingers, her eyes widened. "I've got big hands."

"Vixa has prepared your horses," Tannis said. "Once you have the queen's promise, use this." He handed Vixa a shimmering cube. "It's a magic crystal. Smash it and it will return you here. Bring me good news."

The king moaned again. His crown slipped down his forehead.

"Bring *us* good news," Tannis corrected himself. "Return peace to the Kingdom of Bissel. Return honor to the throne of King Ledipus."

Vixa bowed, turned, and marched from the throne room. Evan and Cleo did the same.

As Vixa silently led them out of the castle gates toward the stables, Cleo turned a cartwheel.

"Being a rogue is kind of nice," she said. "I feel stronger and faster."

"I wish *I* felt different," Evan said.

"What do you mean?"

Evan patted his pocket and pulled out a slender wand. The handle was wrapped in braided leather. He swished the tip of his wand through the air. Green sparks crackled out.

"I have no idea how to use this thing," he said. "If I have to cast a spell, I think we're in trouble."

JOIN THE RACE!

It's an incredible adventure through the animal kingdom, as kids zip-line, kayak, and scuba dive their way to the finish line! Packed with cool facts about amazing creatures, dangerous habitats, and more!

■SCHOLASTIC

scholastic.com

MEET RANGER

A time–traveling golden retriever with search-and-rescue training . . . and a nose for danger!